A VERY WOMPKEE CHRISTMAS

Story book adapted by Mark Medford
from a screenplay by Peter Hunziker and Cynthia Riddle.
The Wompkees are a creation of Con Fullam and Maura Clarke.

C·5 Books

NEW YORK, NY

Computer Illustrations By
Chris Allard, Jamie Norton, Ed Brillant,
Heather Shipman, Aren Voorhees, Glen Whelden.

Images copyright © 2003 Deos Animation Studios

© 2003 Wompkee is a registered trademark of Wompkee LLC

Book Design By HRoberts Design.

Printed in Singapore.

First Edition
ISBN 1-59315-010-5
Library of Congress Cataloging-in-Publication data available upon request.

Wompkee Wood is a magical place full of wonderful Wompkees! Wompkees are friendly and brave. They love to sing, go on adventures, and pick Wompberries. Wompberries are *very, very* important!

Wompberries make the Puffer Steamers work and the Puffer Steamers make *everything* work! Wompkees have really BIG ears. With them, Wompkees can slide down a Shoot Chute and fly! Every Wompkee, that is, except for one. Little Twig. Her ears are just too small.

"Tonight is the Christmas Eve Festival," sighed Twig, "and I want to put the star on top of the tree!"

But it was a very tall tree, and so she would have to learn to fly *today*. "I know, that will be my Christmas wish!" Twig tugged her furry ears. "Come . . . on . . . ears . . . S-T-R-E-T-C-H!"

They felt a *little* bigger. HOP! Into the Shoot Chute she went. POP! Out she came, flapping her ears. "Oh, no," she cried. Twig ran out of flaps and flopped right into a pile of snow!

In the Great Hall, Daisy, Scout, Hummer, Buster, and Gran ate breakfast. Gran was the oldest and wisest Wompkee. "Who gets to put the star on top of the tree, Gran?" asked Daisy.

In walked Twig. "Me!" she said. The Wompkees all shook their heads. "Maybe next year," said Hummer, "when your ears are bigger." Twig was sad.

She sat on Gran's lap. "When your heart is ready, and your wish is true," Gran whispered, "then you'll fly." "But I want to fly *now*," sniffed Twig. "Waiting takes too long!" Gran handed her a broom. "While you're waiting, you can help me clean!"

The other Wompkees were so busy getting ready for the Christmas Eve Festival, that they didn't see the evil Ice Fairies.

The Ice Fairies were busy, too: stealing Wompberries for Iglora Borealis, the Ice Queen!

Iglora and her dog, Woofus, lived in an ice cave at the very top of Rocky Crag. Iglora hated everything that was warm and snuggly *especially* Wompkees! The Ice Queen needed Wompberries for her Ice Device. In went Wompberries; out came snow. She wanted to freeze Wompkee Wood!

The only thing Iglora hated more than Wompkees was the Wompberry bush that grew outside her cave. It was full of Wompberries, but it wouldn't let her or Woofus pick any!

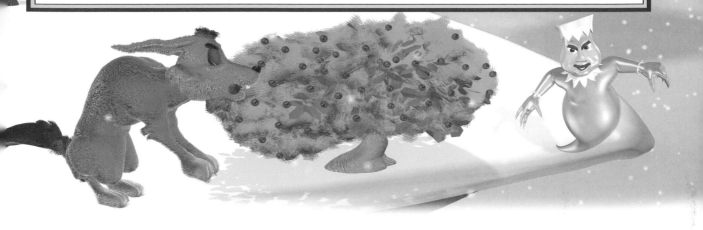

Only Wompkees could pick Wompberries.
"WOOFUS!" screamed Iglora. "Get me a Wompkee!"

"I want to put up lights and bake Wompberry pies, too," complained Twig. "Cleaning isn't fun!" When Gran fell asleep, she snuck down the Shoot Chute.

"Hmmmm . . ." said Hummer, looking at his weather machine. The Whizzer Dial said "Sunny". It was cloudy. The Flake-O-Meter was on zero. It was snowing. "Better get inside," he warned. "There's a HUGE storm coming!" "Wait!" called Scout. "Bring Wompberries for the Puffer Steamers. If they stop puffing, Wompkee Wood will freeze!"

Scout looked in the bin. The Wompberries were…GONE! "Stolen!" said Daisy. "Ice Fairies!" scowled Buster.

The Wompkees went to tell Gran the bad news. She'd know what to do!

"You'll have to get some more," she said. "But *be careful*. That Iglora Borealis is up to something!"

"I want to go, too," said Twig bravely. "Iglora doesn't scare me!" "No, Twig," said Scout. "You're too—"

"Little?!" Twig said, making a face.

"Little," agreed Scout. And Twig stomped off.

"Where do you think *she's* going?" asked Daisy. "I don't know," answered Hummer. He looked up at Rocky Crag. "But I know where *we're* going." They walked through the Ice Forest and skated across Great Womp Lake.

Soon they were standing at the bottom of Rocky Crag. "It's s-s-s-scary," said Buster. SNAP! "W-h-h-at was that?!" asked Daisy. "Hmmmm . . .," said Hummer. "Probably just a twig." Hummer was right. It was little Twig—she following them!

Woofus hid behind a rock with a big cane! "Here's the Wompberry bush!" shouted Daisy. Woofus peeked out. There were four Wompkees picking Wompberries!

"My bucket's full," called Scout. "I can fit one more," Buster said. "That big one WAY up . . ." Buster slipped and tumbled over Rocky Crag! SWOOP! Down came Woofus' cane, but it was too late! Flapping their ears, the Wompkees and the Wompberries headed for home.

"You let them get away!" Iglora screeched at Woofus. He hung his shaggy head. "Ice Fairies," she ordered. "GO GET THEM!"

Back in the ice forest, Twig was lost. She started singing loudly. "Maybe someone will hear me," she thought. Someone did: Woofus! "Hello, little Wompkee," Woofus said in his nicest voice. "Eeeeek!" They both jumped. "We scared each other!" laughed Twig. "My name's Woofus. What's yours?" "Twig," answered the Wompkee. "And I'm c-c-cold!"

"My cave is warm," said Woofus. "I'll take you there!" Along the way, Twig told Woofus all about her Christmas wish.

Back near Wompkee Wood, Ice Fairies chased the Wompkees! "Zigzag!" yelled Scout. He zipped through the trees, twisting and turning. The Ice Fairies were too slow. BOING! BOING! BOING! They got stuck in the trees!

"Just in time," puffed Buster. "Look!" The lights in Wompkee Wood were flickering out. Daisy reached into her bucket. "My Wompberries are gone!" "Mine, too!" said Hummer. They had all spilled during the chase.

Back in Woofus's cave, it wasn't warm at all. Everything was made of ice! Iglora floated in. "Who are you?" asked Twig. "Why, I'm Woofus's auntie," Iglora replied.

Twig's tummy grumbled. On the floor was a big bucket of Wompberries.

She popped one in her mouth. "Don't EAT them!" screamed Iglora.

"I can pick you some more," Twig offered. "There's a bush right outside."

"Oh please, pick me *lots* more!" said the Ice Queen.

"Oh, my!" cried Gran. "Where is my little Twig?!"
The Puffer Steamers stopped puffing. The lights
went out. Scout told Gran about the Ice Fairies.
"Twig must have followed you!" she said. Little
Twig was in BIG trouble. They had to rescue
her! "But we can't fly in this *awful* storm,"
sighed Buster.

Hummer had an idea. With an old Puffer Steamer
and two waterwheels, he built a Steamer Roller.
"Now, that's what I call Womp-power!" shouted Daisy.
They rumbled through the Ice Forest.

"I-I-I-I don't know about this," said Buster. The Steamer Roller started climbing up Rocky Crag. Then—it got stuck. "Grab that branch!" yelled Scout. The Wompkees all jumped—just in time! C R A S H went the Steamer Roller!

The Ice Device stopped working. The snowstorm ended. "It's out of Wompberries!" screeched Iglora. Twig thought everything looked beautiful. "Auntie," she said. "I want to go home now." "Not until you get me MORE Wompberries!" snapped Iglora.

Just then, Buster, Scout, and Daisy hopped over the ledge.

"It's th-th-th-the Ice Queen!" Buster shouted. Daisy and Scout grabbed Twig by the ears and took off! "Stop them, Woofus!" Iglora screeched. "She has *my* Wompberries!"

But there was nothing Woofus could do.

That night, as Twig sat on her bed, *trying* to stay out of trouble, Ice Fairies flew by her window. They were stealing the Wompberries again! Twig jumped down the Shoot Chute, remembering Gran's words: *"When your heart is ready, and your wish is true, then you'll fly."*

"I want to save Wompkee Wood! " she wished.
And she started flying! "Wheee . . .Zowie . . .!"

"Look!" Hummer pointed. "Twig's flying!" She
was chasing Ice Fairies and it looked like she
needed help! The Wompkees held hands,
spinning around and around. They started to
glow! Wompkee Wood got so warm that all of
the Ice Fairies melted!

Woofus had never seen the Ice Queen so angry! He ran out of the cave and right into the warm glow of Wompkee Wood. Iglora chased him and she melted into a puddle!

When the cold came back, she froze like a big pancake! "See you around," chuckled Woofus.

"Woofus?" Someone was calling him. "Up here!" Twig was flying! Woofus looked sad.
"Let's spend Christmas together," she said, giving him a big hug. Woofus smiled.

"Twig saved Wompkee Wood!" the Wompkees cheered. "That's right," said Gran, handing her the Christmas star. Twig could hardly believe it! She flew to the top of the big tree. Carefully she put the star on. When she did, all of the Christmas lights twinkled brightly!

That night everything was peaceful in Wompkee Wood. The Puffer Steamers puffed. Night-lights glowed. And one little Wompkee got her Christmas wish!

THE END

DREAMS CAN COME TRUE!

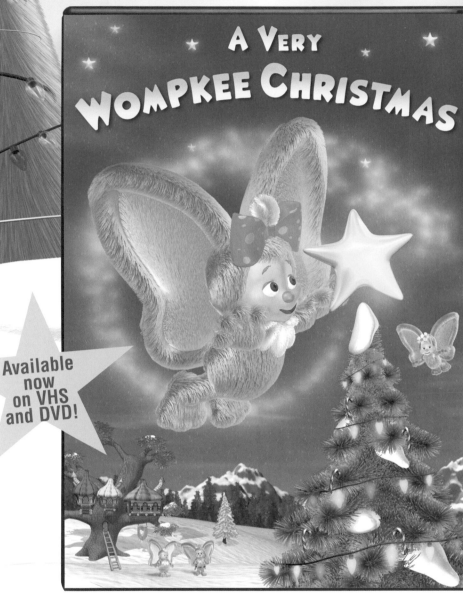

A VERY Wompkee Christmas

Available now on VHS and DVD!

JOIN TWIG AS SHE GETS HER CHRISTMAS WISH
JUST IN TIME TO SAVE WOMPKEE WOOD!

DVD SPECIAL FEATURES INCLUDE:
- **Three Animated Christmas Videos**
- **'Live' Wompkee Portrait Paintings by Award-winning Artist**
- **Wompkee Family Bios**

Wompkee plush toy items are available at your favorite gift shop.

LOOK FOR **A VERY WOMPKEE CHRISTMAS** ON
VHS AND DVD WHEREVER VIDEOS ARE SOLD!

deos WOMPKEE LLC

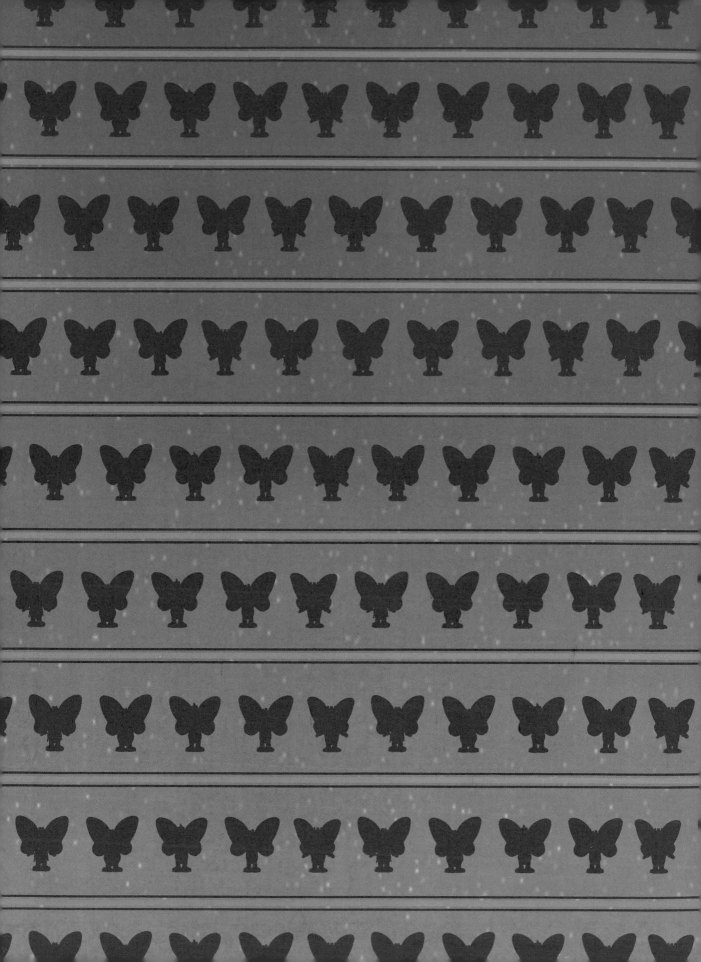